Chapter 1

TOM TURNER HAD lived in a town all his life, in a tiny flat with no garden and nowhere to kick a football except, secretly, in his bedroom, and that had been banned after he'd accidentally kicked the ball through his window.

Then Tom's father became Headmaster of Appleford Primary School, and the Turner family had to move miles away into the country.

Mr Turner went first. He stayed in the village while he looked for a new home for his family. Two miles outside Appleford, he found Hazel Cottage, surrounded by woods and fields. It needed a coat of paint and a bit of work doing on the garden, but otherwise, it was perfect.

Half-way through the summer term, Mrs Turner, Tom and his younger sister Daisy boarded the train to Appleford. Daisy was cross all the way; she'd had to leave her pretty yellow bedroom and her best friend, Annabelle, behind. Tom wasn't sure how he felt. He reckoned the country would be all right if he could find a friend.

"It won't be easy at first," their father warned them, "but once you've got used to it, you'll love it!"

Would they ever get used to it, Tom wondered? He couldn't sleep that first night in Hazel Cottage. He stood by his open window, amazed by the vast emptiness of the countryside. There was only one house in view: a big red farmhouse with an orchard beside it, where sheep moved in the moonlight. Beyond the farm an eerie orange glow indicated the village of Appleford, but the cottage itself was enveloped in a vast soundless cloak, that spread over the tangled garden and out into the distant hills.

And then, in a field beyond the lane, a dark form moved, swift and graceful beside the hedge. It vanished into the trees and a small scream dwindled to silence in the wood.

The new school was even stranger than the new home. There were only three classes and three teachers. In Tom's last school there had been many, many more.

"This is Tom Turner," Mrs Gates introduced him to her class. "His father is our new headmaster." She

lead Tom to a seat beside a boy with a mop of black curly hair.

"And this is Glyn Bowen," she told Tom. "He lives near you, at Orchard Farm."

Glyn didn't look up.

Tom felt odd and uncomfortable. Children turned to stare at him. But

their attention was diverted by the late arrival of a big boy who clattered into the classroom ten minutes late.

"And what kept you this time, Brian Moody?" asked Mrs Gates.

"An old fox has been and got our chickens, Mrs Gates," said Brian. "There was a right mess. A vixen it was. Our old hound Bugle caught her; killed her he did; but there's cubs and we've been looking for them."

"It's mean to kill cubs," Tom's curly-headed neighbour suddenly spoke up. "If your dad locked his chickens in safe at night, the foxes wouldn't get them."

"That's all you know, Glyn Bowen," snarled Brian. "Cubs are a pest, same as foxes. My brother Jo'll get them, even if the old hound doesn't!"

"Your brother's a wimp!" Glyn

flung at the big boy, and everybody laughed.

"If I hear another word from you two, you'll both go to the headmaster," Mrs Gates warned.

Everyone looked at Tom.

There was peace until break, then gangs were formed. Brian Moody's gang murmured under a chestnut tree. Glyn and his friends kicked a football round the playground. The girls separated into groups of two and three, only Daisy stood alone in her pale-pink dress. Tom tried to avoid her. He felt a bit mean but she looked as though she was going to someone's party, with a big pink bow in her curls.

Glyn Bowen came towards Tom, dribbling a football. "Can I play?" Tom asked.

"Out of the way, townie!" said a boy

in Glyn's gang.

Tom stood aside. Dad was right. It wasn't going to be easy. If only his father wasn't the headmaster. If only Daisy didn't look like Alice in Wonderland.

Mrs Turner was busy that week; she painted the gate, cut down the nettles and bought Daisy some jeans in the local market, so she'd look like the other girls in the village. Daisy wouldn't wear them.

Tom didn't know what to do in the long afternoons when school was over. He'd read all his comics twice, couldn't play football by himself, and was fed up with toys. He wanted an adventure.

One evening he decided to explore the woods behind Hazel Cottage. It was eerie beneath the trees; wild and shadowy, not at all like a town park. He hadn't ventured far when he came upon a little stone house. It was quite deserted and most of the slates had

fallen off the roof, but the walls were still intact. There was even a very old table in a tiny room under the remaining part of the roof. Tom wondered who had lived there, long ago, when there was no electricity and no television. There wasn't even a road to the house. He thought about bringing a friend there, one day, to share a picnic. It was such a safe and secret place.

When he got home Mrs Turner had news for him. "The Bowens have invited us to tea on Saturday," she told Tom. "Glyn's just your age, isn't he? And his sister's in Daisy's class. You'll have a good time."

"I hope Daisy doesn't wear her pink dress!" Tom said.

She did.

"You look like a raspberry ice-cream," Tom muttered when she got into the car.

Mr Turner overheard and said, "Tom, that sort of remark isn't going to help."

"Nothing's going to help," Tom retorted.

Tea was in the garden at the back of the farmhouse; the most delicious spread Tom had ever seen. Mrs Bowen was round and jolly, her husband thin and jolly with a wrinkled weatherbeaten face and black hair like Glyn's. Tom liked them.

Megan Bowen giggled and nudged her brother when she saw Daisy. Glyn made a face and Tom found he had a knot in his stomach that wouldn't go away, and he had to say, 'No thank you,' when it came to the cake. He'd always loved fruit cake and he hated

Daisy for wearing those beads and bows.

After tea the children were told to run away and play. Glyn and Megan ran away all right. They disappeared into the thick lattice of grass and nettles that fringed the orchard.

Tom plunged after them. "Come on, Daisy," he cried. "I think we're

supposed to be playing hide-and-seek."

Daisy would come no further than the first nettle. "I'll spoil my dress," she wailed.

"Go back to Mum, then," Tom hissed. "I'll sort this lot out."

He pushed his way through the undergrowth, too angry to care about thorns and stinging nettles, and then he was in a wood. Beneath the trees, the weeds were less dense and he gathered speed as he leapt into the maze of branches. Megan darted from a bush and Tom flung himself at her. Caught off balance, Megan tumbled into a ditch. Tom waited for tears, but Megan glared at him, rubbing her elbows, and said, "You haven't won yet. You've got to catch Glyn."

"OK, if those are your rules," Tom said. "We play fair where I come from.

The first one caught is 'on'."

Megan glowered.

Tom ran on; he'd delayed too long. Glyn had vanished. The trees began to thin as they mounted a steep incline covered in last winter's leaves. Tom's feet slipped and he had to grab at roots and branches to stop himself from sliding all the way back. And then he found himself standing at the edge of the wood and looking about across a vast green plain, to where mountains

rose, like huge misty blue pyramids.

He forgot the chase and stood staring at the mountains until a twig snapped and he turned to see Glyn standing, almost behind him, flat against a tree.

Tom leapt, his hands shot out and he touched Glyn's curly head. "Got you!" Tom cried.

The two boys watched each other. Tom wondered what the rules were now. Glyn seemed uncertain, so Tom said, "What are those mountains?"

"That's Wales," said Glyn. "It's a different country. My dad comes from there. They're the oldest mountains in the world."

Tom looked at the misty blue pyramids.

"You'd better get going," Glyn reminded him, "or I'll catch you before you've started. I'll count three and give you a chance."

So their rules were almost the same. Tom bounded down the bank and into the trees again. He'd always been a good runner and he reached the tea-table seconds before Glyn.

"He didn't catch me," Tom shouted breathlessly as he clung to the table.

"You look as though you've had a good time," his father remarked, glancing at Tom's scratched arms and torn T-shirt.

"Great!" Tom said, looking round, but Glyn had gone again.

Mrs Bowen took the Turners on a tour. Tom saw Glyn's room, he saw his telescope, his cat and his bike, but Glyn had vanished. And Tom thought they had almost been friends out in the wood.

"I'll give him a good talking-to when he turns up," said Mrs Bowen, "He shouldn't disappear like this when friends come visiting. I'm afraid Glyn's taken against teachers," she explained. "He was always in trouble with the last headmaster – used to come home, eyes red with tears. He was slow to read, you see, and he's proud."

So that was it! Didn't Glyn understand that this headmaster was different?

When they left the farmhouse Glyn and Megan still had not put in an appearance.

"You must come over to Hazel Cottage," Mrs Turner invited, just before they drove off. "I get lonely in the day, with all of them out at school."

Tom noticed Glyn and Megan

creeping round the side of the house.

"You should get a dog," Mrs Bowen said, "They're good company."

"We've got a canary," Daisy sang out.

Megan tittered.

Tom shoved his elbow into Daisy's ice-cream dress. He didn't mean to hurt, but Daisy howled.

"Tom, what did you do?" Mrs Turner demanded, while her husband revved the engine louder than usual, mercifully drowning Daisy's howls.

"I thought you and Glyn had made friends," Mr Turner said when they got home.

"No, Dad. I'm not anybody's friend," Tom replied and he ran upstairs.

When he looked out across the fields that night, he saw something moving through the long grass. This time it was not the graceful shape of a running creature, it was a boy with something in his arms, stepping stealthily through the moonlight, like a thief with a bundle of gold.

Chapter 2

"I'VE GOT TO go to London next Saturday," Mr Turner informed them a few days later, "to buy some books. D'you want anything?"

"Pink trainers," said Daisy, "size 12, please. If I've got to wear trainers I want pink ones."

Tom groaned.

"What about you, Tom?" Mr Turner asked.

"Nothing," Tom said. Friends could not be put into bags and carried home.

"A book about space?" Mr Turner suggested.

"All right!" Tom replied, without enthusiasm. Glyn had not spoken to him since they'd visited his house. No one had spoken to him except Brian Moody who'd told him to, 'Get out of it, townie!' when he'd tried to grab the football.

Mr Turner set off early on Saturday morning. He was to stay the night with his brother, Uncle Harry, and return on Sunday.

From his bedroom window, Tom watched the car sliding away up the lane. Its shiny white roof was still in sight when the doorbell rang.

Tom heard his mother talking on the doorstep and a boy's voice answer her. He ran downstairs and saw Glyn and Megan standing by the front door.

"They've brought us a puppy, Tom," said Mrs Turner. "I think you'd better take care of it, I don't know much about these things."

"But it's for you," Megan said, "from our Mum; she said it would keep you company."

"That's very kind of her," Mrs Turner looked uncertain. "It's . . . it's an odd sort of dog!"

"Part corgi," Glyn explained. "Mum got it off a friend."

"I see," Mrs Turner wiped her wet hands anxiously on her apron and regarded the bundle in Glyn's arms.

Tom saw a small pointed face peeping out of Glyn's anorak. He saw uneasy amber-coloured eyes and he knew it was not a puppy. Anger boiled up in him. How dare they think he was too stupid to know a fox when he saw one. How dare they trick his mother because she had never lived in the

country, and trusted the Bowens. He was about to shout, "That's a fox," when he suddenly thought better of it and said instead, "I'll take the puppy."

Glyn brought the little creature out of his anorak. It struggled and made a funny frightened sound in the back of its throat.

Daisy appeared and cried, "Oh, what a sweet dog. Can I hold it?"

"No," said Tom. "It might bite. I'm going to put it in the garden shed."

"Yes, I think that would be best for now," his mother agreed. "Would you two like to come in for a bit?" she asked the Bowens.

"No thanks!" Glyn turned away as he answered and he and Megan ran down the path.

Megan began to titter as she closed the gate.

"That girl's always laughing," Daisy remarked. She followed Tom to the garden shed.

"Close the door," Tom said when they were inside. "The puppy might run away."

"What shall we call him?" Daisy asked. "He's a funny colour."

"How about Rufus?" The name sprang automatically into his mind. He'd remembered Dad telling him once that Rufus meant red, or a sort of red.

"That's a good name. You are clever, Tom!"

Daisy was all right sometimes, Tom had to admit. He put Rufus on the floor, but the little animal seemed unsteady on his feet. He was very thin and his lovely red-brown coat was matted with mud. He stared at Tom with his mysterious golden eyes, then he limped across to a low shelf where Mrs Turner kept trays of seedlings.

"He's hurt!" Tom observed. "Look, he's dragging his back leg."

"Oh, the poor little thing!" Daisy crouched beside Rufus and put out her hand.

The cub's lip curled back, revealing a row of sharp little teeth. He backed into the darkness beneath the shelf, then turned his face to the wall.

"He's frightened!" Tom said.

"What shall we do? How can we make him better?" Daisy knelt on the dusty floor, unconcerned for her new white skirt.

"Perhaps he's thirsty. Get him some water, Daisy," Tom suggested.

"That's a good idea. I always like a drink when I'm scared." Daisy was gone in a flash.

The little foxcub hunched himself further into the dark. Tom wanted to stroke it but was uncertain. Dogs and cats liked to be petted but this was a wild animal. It only seemed to want to escape from him. But if they let the cub go, limping like that, Brian Moody's old hound would probably get it, or even worse, Brian's brother with his gun. Perhaps the vixen that Bugle killed was this cub's mother.

"You'll have to stay here for a bit, Rufus," Tom said gently. "When you're strong and your leg is better, I'll let you go."

Daisy came in with one of the best blue cereal bowls.

"Does Mum know?" Tom asked.

"She's busy," Daisy replied, "and I couldn't find anything else."

Tom placed the bowl beside Rufus, but the cub just shuffled away from it.

"He's still frightened," Tom said.

"Perhaps he'll drink when he's alone. Let's go and get him some meat."

"There's only mince," Mrs Turner told her son. "And that's for shepherd's pie, tonight."

"Just a bit," Tom pleaded. "The puppy's very hungry and I'm not, and Daisy never finishes her shepherd's pie."

"Well . . . I suppose . . ."

Tom went to the fridge before his mother could change her mind. He took two large spoonfuls of mince, put it on a saucer and ran down to the shed.

Daisy had beaten him to it. She was lying on the floor, half under the shelf. Tom put the mince beside Rufus and the cub nuzzled the saucer with the tip of his black nose. For a few moments he sniffed the meat suspiciously, then, all at once, he began to eat, gulping

the mince down in hungry mouthfuls.

Tom felt so relieved and, somehow, excited. If only Daisy knew that they were feeding a wild animal. But he dared not tell her yet. And what if Dad found out. If Mr Turner knew that Glyn had tricked them into taking a foxcub, he would be angry. Glyn would be in trouble and Tom didn't want that to happen. He would have to find a way of keeping the fox a secret from his father.

The problem was resolved next morning when Tom woke very early, too early. He wondered why he had woken, and then he heard the bark, or rather growl, low and hungry-sounding, coming from the back of the house.

Tom got out of bed and ran to the bathroom; the only room, apart from

Daisy's, with a window overlooking the back garden.

There, pacing up and down beside the shed, was a large unfriendly-looking brown and white dog.

"Oh no!" Tom said aloud. "It must be Brian Moody's old hound!"

Chapter 3

THE BIG DOG had obviously smelt a fox and he wasn't going to move until he'd got it.

"No! No! No!" Tom moaned. But, of course, that didn't help. He would have to do something positive. There were two problems to resolve. How to get the dog away from the shed; how to get the foxcub out and where to put it when this had been achieved.

Tom considered for a moment, then, fairly confident that he had found two answers, he quickly slipped back to his room, put on his jeans, T-shirt and trainers, grabbed his schoolbag, and crept downstairs to the kitchen.

He opened the fridge door. The mince was all gone but a shoulder of lamb sat on a plate on the top shelf, all ready for the Sunday roast. He couldn't take all of it, he realised, but just a bit wouldn't show.

Tom found a carving knife, took the joint out of the fridge and cut a large slice from it; this he wrapped in an old crisp packet he found in his schoolbag. Having replaced the joint, he was about to shut the fridge door when a plastic box caught his eye: leftovers from the shepherd's pie. He put the box into his bag on top of the lamb.

Brian Moody's hound began to bark again, louder than ever.

Tom took his father's oilskin jacket

from a peg in the hall and opened the back door. He came face to face with the meanest dog he'd ever seen.

"Well, you're not going to get my fox," Tom snarled at the dog. He drew the lamb out of his bag and held it out. The hound's nose twitched and he moved closer. Tom ran round to the front garden as fast as he could; the dog followed, his jaws open now and showing wicked yellow teeth. Brian Moody might have been proud of that dog but he didn't feed it too well, Tom thought. It looked as though it hadn't had a decent meal for days.

All at once, the big dog leapt at Tom, but the boy reeled back and flung the meat as far as he could over the road, over the hedge and into the field beyond.

The huge dog gave a furious howling

snarl, jumped over the Turners' gate, rushed across the road and squeezed himself through the hedge where he presumably pounced on the meat, for his howl became a deep satisfied grunting.

Tom tore back to the shed. Inside, the fox, terrified by the sound and the scent of a hound, was huddled in the dark, his fur bristling, his teeth bared. Tom didn't have time to be afraid. He flung his father's jacket over the little creature and bundled him into the bag. Then he darted out of the shed, across the vegetable patch and threw himself over the fence at the back. He was in the wood now, the house and a road lay between him and the hound. If he was lucky the old dog would be too busy to think about foxes until they were well out of earshot.

Tom could feel his heart thumping as he ran through the wood. He was a

little scared of what he was doing: running alone through a silent wood, long before breakfast, with Mum not knowing where he was. But one thing he was sure of; he had to save Rufus and he had to keep him secret.

He came to the stone house sooner than he expected. He must have run very fast. Tom wrenched open the door. It was extraordinary, and so lucky, that the thick oak door had remained, while the roof had all but rotted away. The little cub would have a carpet of moss and cobbles, sky and branches above his head, and four high stone walls to keep him safe.

Tom went into the small room at the end of the stone house, where the roof still remained. A few tiles were missing but it was dark and dry in the corner where the table stood. Tom knelt down and gently removed the bundle from his bag. The foxcub rolled out of Mr Turner's jacket and lay glaring at Tom.

"I know you're frightened and your leg hurts," Tom said. "But I wish you could like me, I'm trying to help." He took out the plastic box, opened it and placed it beside the cub.

Still glaring, and making a strange, angry noise, the cub edged closer to the cold shepherd's pie. He was

confused and terrified after his undignified journey, but he was hungry too. He began to eat.

Tom crawled away. "I'll be back," he said. "I promise!"

When he left the stone house he could hear the cub pushing the box of food across the cobbled floor. Tom closed the door behind him, giving an extra firm tug to make sure no other animal could invade the foxcub's new home.

His mother was up when he got back. "Where on earth have you been?" she cried, eyeing his dew-wet shoes and tousled hair, "and what have you been doing?"

"Puppy got out!" Tom explained. "I tried to catch it, but it's gone."

"Someone's taken a slice of my lamb joint," Mrs Turner complained. "Was that you?"

"Yes! For the puppy!"

"And the shepherd's pie?" she went on incredulously.

"Yes! The puppy was hungry!" Tom tried to look innocent.

"I can't believe it. That was enough meat to feed ten puppies, I'd have thought!"

"We-e-ell . . ." Tom wriggled. "I took a bit extra to lure him back!"

Mrs Turner raised her eyebrows. "We'd better ring the police," she said. "That puppy might be valuable."

"I wouldn't do that, Mum!" Tom said quickly. "Police don't like to be bothered with silly things like puppies."

"But Mrs Bowen gave him to us. I wouldn't want her to think we didn't care." His mother began to dust leaves from his hair. "Still, perhaps we'd better wait until your dad gets home, he'll know what to do."

"Yes, Dad'll know," Tom said thankfully. "And the puppy might come back."

Daisy was distraught when she heard that Rufus had vanished. "He was hurt," she cried. "He'll get run over!"

"No, he won't," said Tom. "I know he won't!"

Mr Turner was home in time to eat what was left of the lamb. He was intrigued to hear of the strange puppy's appearance and rapid disappearance. "It's sounds rather special," he said. "If it doesn't turn up by tomorrow, I'll ring the police."

"We'd better let Mrs Bowen know," added his wife. "This afternoon I'll go and thank her for sending the puppy over. Do you want to come, children?"

Tom shook his head but Daisy cried, "I'll come!"

Tom and his father had just settled down to watch cricket on television when the car returned and they heard Daisy running up the path shouting,

"Guess what? Guess what?"

"What?" asked Tom as Daisy burst into the room.

"Mrs Bowen never sent that puppy. It must have been a stray, she says, that's why it was all thin and muddy. That horrid Glyn got ever such a row for playing a trick like that."

For some reason Tom felt sorry for Glyn.

"Well, that's that," said Mr Turner. "No sense in bothering the police about a stray."

It suddenly occured to Tom that Glyn might have been trying to protect the cub when he gave it to them. He remembered how angrily Glyn had defended foxes when Brian Moody had boasted of his old hound killing the vixen. Perhaps Rufus was her cub.

For the moment the little fox was

safe in the wood, but how was Tom going to feed it, day after day, until it was strong enough to fend for itself? It was already half-starved, if it didn't get food the cub would surely die.

Chapter 4

"WHERE'S MY OILSKIN jacket?" Tom heard his father ask that evening. "I'm sure I left it on this peg."

Mrs Turner was helping Tom sort out pieces of puzzle on the kitchen table. "It wasn't there this morning," she said. "Perhaps it's in the car."

"I've looked!" Mr Turner was irritated. He wanted some exercise; a walk to the post box, but it had begun to rain. "I'll have another look in the boot."

Tom dropped two pieces of sky on to the floor. He had remembered where the jacket was.

His mother went upstairs to search. Tom seized his opportunity. He opened the fridge as quietly as he could; there wasn't much lamb left, it would be too obvious if he took that. What else would a fox eat? Eggs? Frozen peas? Cheese?

"I'll have a look in the kitchen!" Mr Turner's voice was too near.

Tom grabbed the packet of cheese, slid it into his pocket and slammed the fridge door, just as his father came into the room. "Dad, I've remembered something," he said. "I sort of borrowed your jacket when I went to look for the puppy."

"Borrowed it?" Mr Turner looked suspicious.

"Yes, I was in a hurry, you see, so I took your coat because it was nearer than mine and I must have left it in the woods."

"Tom, that jacket was new. What's the matter with you?"

"I'll go and get it, Dad. I know just where it is," Tom said eagerly.

"I'd better come with you," Mr Turner sighed.

"No! No, don't do that! I'll run!" And run he did, through the garden, over the fence and into the woods, while Mr Turner stood at the back door, wondering whether to be anxious or angry.

Tom raced through the trees. A narrow path was taking shape where his feet flattened the undergrowth. It made his passage easier, but would someone else find the path, and follow it to the stone house?

The cub was lying in darkness under

the table, his head and paws resting on the warm lining of the oilskin jacket. "I'm sorry," said Tom as he gently removed the jacket. The little fox grunted. Tom unwrapped the cheese and pushed it towards the cub. Rufus looked at the unfamiliar cube of pale yellow. He sniffed it and looked at Tom.

"I'll have to go now or someone'll come and find you," Tom told Rufus. "But I'll be back tomorrow. Go on, you eat that cheese and you'll feel better."

Could he keep his promise? Tom was so worried he was hardly aware of the rain splashing through the trees on to his bare head, or the grass that brushed against his legs, soaking his jeans to the knee.

"Whatever's got into you, Tom?"

asked his mother when he appeared in the kitchen, dripping on to her clean floor. "Leaving your dad's jacket in the wood. I don't know!"

Tom handed her the jacket.

"It smells peculiar," Daisy remarked, eyeing the jacket suspiciously. Did she guess? Rufus did have rather a strong smell about him.

"You *look* peculiar!" Tom retorted. He rushed out before Daisy could think of a reply.

She did look peculiar though, with four white bows stuck on top of her head. Tom hoped she wouldn't wear the bows in school next day.

She did!

Tom saw Megan Bowen and her friends laughing behind Daisy's back. Daisy didn't seem to care.

After tea, that evening, Tom went upstairs to read a book he'd found in the school library; it was about British wildlife. He thought he might learn what foxcubs should eat and how often, and what to do with lame animals. He'd hardly opened the book, however, when Daisy poked her head round his door.

"What d'you want?" asked Tom, slamming the book shut.

"Nothing," said Daisy timidly. "I just wondered if we should go and look for that puppy?"

"We'd never find him!" Tom said.

"I wish he'd come back, don't you?" Daisy sounded so sad, Tom almost forgave her for wearing the bows to school.

"What's that book about?" she asked, moving cautiously into the room.

"Just a book, now go away and play with your dolls or something. Oh, and by the way," Tom added, "the girls in school were laughing at you today."

"Why?" A hurt frown creased Daisy's pretty pink features.

"Those bows!" Tom said.

"D'you think I shouldn't wear them?"

"'Course you shouldn't, not to school anyway. And why must you wear that soppy dress every day?"

"I like it!" Daisy glared at Tom, trying to hold back an offended sob. She withdrew, slamming the door behind her and shouting through it, "You're mean!"

Advice was all very well he realised, but only in small doses. He returned to his book. Half an hour later he had learnt that foxcubs were born in spring and drank their mother's milk. When they were weaned they ate small rodents, worms and anything they could get. Urban foxes even ate biscuits and bread. Tom couldn't guess how old Rufus was. He could have been ten weeks or more than three months old. "I'll try and get some biscuits to him," Tom said to himself.

His parents were busy in the garden. Daisy had shut herself in her room.

Tom went into the kitchen and found a packet of chocolate biscuits. He was about to put them in his pocket when his mother walked in.

"Where are you going with those?" she inquired.

"Just to the wood. I was taking them in case I got hungry."

"No, you don't," said his mother. "Those are all that are left. Put them back."

"Cake?" Tom asked, hopefully.

"You had it all for tea. And while we're on the subject of food, did you take half a pound of cheese yesterday?"

"Yes!" Tom began to shuffle backwards.

"All of it?"

"Yes!"

"Tom, really. You get a big school dinner!"

"I'm growing," Tom said defensively, and fled.

It wasn't his lucky day. His father insisted that he should help with the bonfire instead of playing in the wood. It was a beautiful bonfire. On any other occasion the scent of burning leaves, the jumble of glowing twigs and weeds would have been wonderful entertainment, but while Tom watched the bright sparks drifting into the sky, he thought of the lonely foxcub. He would be without food that night!

Chapter 5

TOM HAD KEPT out of Brian Moody's way as much as he could since that first day at school. But his preoccupation with Rufus caused him to be forgetful.

When he crossed the playground next day he was unaware that he was walking right into the path of a carefully aimed football.

"Out of the way, boy!" yelled Brian Moody.

Confused, Tom turned and stared at Brian. The football bounced into his ankle and straight on to the toe of

Brian's opponent.

"You idiot!" Brian thundered towards Tom. "Get out of it!"

"Get out of it yourself!" Tom shook his fist at Brian.

It was a risky thing to do. Too risky! Brian landed a right hook on Tom's cheek. Tom reeled back and struck out wildly. Somehow, he managed to jab Brian in the eye.

"Oooooooow!" The noise Brian made was awful, so was his next assault. He aimed a powerful kick at Tom's knee. Tom toppled to the ground and Brian pounced on him, triumphantly. Tom thought his last hour had come but someone said, "Leave off, you big bully!" And Brian's great weight was lifted away. Tom looked up to see Glyn Bowen dragging Brian across the ground.

In another moment the bully would have been on to Tom again but Glyn whispered, "His dad's coming!"

Mr Turner walked over to the group of boys surrounding Tom and Brian. "What's going on?" he demanded.

"Nothing," said Tom, getting to his feet.

Mr Turner regarded the reddening chin and the swollen eye. "Have you been fighting?" He addressed himself to Brian.

"It was a game," said Tom. "No one got hurt."

"I won't have fighting in my school," said his father. "Is that understood?"

"Yes, sir!" a meek chorus answered him.

"Tom and Brian, go and wash yourselves and get ready for the next lesson." Mr Turner left the playground.

Everyone looked at Tom whose knee was bleeding, and Brian muttered, "He only stopped us because Tom was getting beaten up."

"That's not true!" said Glyn Bowen. "He didn't fuss about Tom's knee did he?" He walked away as though he regretted what he'd said.

Tom wished his father hadn't stopped the fight. He wanted the others to know that he could stand up for himself, and even win, without anyone else's help.

Mr Turner never mentioned the incident at home. He was very good about things like that.

After tea Tom found a large cardboard box. "I'm going to make a den in the wood," he told his mother as he made off with it.

"Can't you play in the garden?" his mother asked.

"No," Tom replied. "Daisy'll get at me. I'm only going the other side of the fence, you can still see me."

Mrs Turner left him to get on with it.

Inside the box, Tom had put an old sweater, a packet of crisps, six slices of bread and butter, a chipped saucer and the remains of Daisy's pork chop, which he had fished out of the compost bin.

He put the cardboard box beside a bramble thicket, within sight of the kitchen window. Then he wrapped the food in his sweater and crept away into the wood. When he could no longer see the cottage, he began to run towards the stone house.

The cub was under the table, exactly where Tom had left him; he was lying on his side and breathing heavily. He must have been lonely and frightened, Tom thought, shut in the stone house for two days without food or water. Perhaps he'd exhausted himself trying to get out? "It's my fault," Tom said to himself. He crawled under the table and drew the cub's head on to his lap. The big amber eyes stared up at him, angry and helpless.

"I'm sorry!" Tom whispered. "I'll come every day after this; I don't care what they say. Only, please don't die!"

He held the chop close to the little animal's nose; Rufus licked it once or twice, then grunted.

Tom tucked his old sweater under the cub's head and went in search of water. At the back of the house a narrow ditch, that he had never noticed, was now gushing with muddy rainwater. Tom dipped the bowl into the ditch until it was full.

When he returned to the cub, Rufus had rolled on to his front and was chewing hungrily at the chop. Tom offered the water and the fox immediately abandoned his bone and gulped down half a bowlful, before returning to his meal of crisps and bread and butter.

When he had finished, the cub allowed Tom to sit close to him and Tom told him about school, about the fight and Glyn Bowen, and about his father. "I think they like my dad, really," he told Rufus. "He's fair and he's a lot nicer than those mean old Moodys."

Tom filled the bowl with water again

before he left. Rufus looked better already, but Tom realised he must never leave him without food or water for such a long time. He laid a few remaining crisps beside the fox and returned, reluctantly, to his cardboard den.

Someone was inside it!

Tom hauled his sister out. "Daisy! That's my den. Can't you mind your own business?" he cried.

"Where've you been?" Daisy asked, sulkily.

"Just for a walk."

"Where?" she persisted.

"It's a secret," Tom said.

"What sort of secret?" Daisy hated other people having secrets.

"What sort? What sort?" Tom groped wildly for an answer. "A red secret," he said, pleased with himself for finding such a neat description of his red-gold friend.

Daisy skulked back to the house.

Before he went to sleep that night, Tom set the alarm on his watch for five o'clock. He wanted to be up very, very early.

The garden was bathed in dewy sunshine when he let himself out of the house next morning. In his schoolbag he had two fish fingers, a packet of biscuits and a hard-boiled egg.

Rufus was better. He had dragged himself out from under the table and didn't growl when Tom approached, nor did he shuffle away.

Tom laid his offerings a few inches away from the fox, then he crouched at a respectful distance and began to talk. He never got a reply, of course, but he felt it was wrong to stare silently at someone who was eating. He returned home at half-past six and crept into bed, ready for his mother to call him at seven. She never guessed he had been up for two hours.

He managed to return to Rufus again, that evening, with three cold sausages and the packet of crisps he'd saved from school. He'd begged his parents to keep Daisy out of his den; so

everyone thought he was there, eating his picnic.

Every morning, for a month, Tom slipped out of the house with a snack for Rufus. And every evening, on the pretext of taking things to his den, he visited the little fox.

Now and again his mother would question him about the food that was disappearing, but Tom always put her at ease with explanations of the enormous appetite that seemed to overcome him after school. Then his father would ask why Tom couldn't stop yawning over breakfast, and Tom would reply that it was the country air and the light nights, and because he was happy and keeping out of trouble, his parents didn't worry.

Sometimes, when Tom helped in the garden, he would gather a pile of worms and stuff them in his pocket. Rufus loved worms!

Slowly, day by day, Rufus grew stronger. Now, when Tom opened the door of the little stone house, he would see the fox basking in a patch of sunshine or limping round, snapping at lazy butterflies. Once or twice Tom found a little pile of earth near the walls, where Rufus had been digging. He wants to be free, Tom thought, but

I daren't let him go yet. He's still not strong enough, and he wondered if the little fox would ever fully recover.

No one ever guessed Tom's secret, and no one ever found the little stone house, not until the first day of the summer holidays. Then, everything happened, all at once!

Chapter 6

ON THE FIRST day of the holiday Tom woke up even before his watch 'beeped' in his ear. He jumped out of bed and slipped into his clothes. It was going to be a wonderful day. No school. He might be able to visit the cub three or four times.

There was a fish pie in the fridge, ready for lunch. He put several spoonfuls into a plastic bag. Would Mrs Turner believe he ate cold fish pie? Too late to wonder. He tidied the remaining pie as best he could before closing the fridge door.

The air was warm, the wood full of birdsong. Tom was enjoying the summer morning so much he didn't hear light footsteps padding after him as he ran through the trees.

Rufus was pleased to see him. He never growled at Tom now, but today he was especially friendly. He limped forward, squeaking with delight. Tom emptied the fish pie on to the saucer and sat back to watch Rufus enjoy his meal. But, suddenly, the little cub backed away, snarling, his fur stood on end and his eyes stared anxiously at something beyond Tom.

Tom looked over his shoulder. Daisy was standing a few feet away from him. "You found the puppy, Tom!" she cried. "Why didn't you tell me?"

"Don't be silly, Daisy!" Tom sighed. "It's not a puppy, it's a fox!"

"A fox?" For a moment Daisy looked panic-stricken, then she asked, "Does he bite?"

"Of course not," Tom reassured his sister. "Not unless you hurt him."

"Is *he* your red secret?"

"Yes."

"But why are you keeping him here?"

Tom told Daisy about Brian Moody's hound and about how he thought his father would be angry if he knew Glyn had given them a foxcub. "I had to keep Rufus somewhere safe, where the hound wouldn't get him," he explained. "You won't tell, will you?"

"'Course not! Poor little thing!" Daisy gazed wistfully at the cub.

Almost as she spoke they heard an awful howling in the distance. Tom couldn't mistake that sound. It was

Brian Moody's hound, and he was coming close. There were shouts, and then a shot: Brian Moody and his brother!

Rufus heard the dog too. He ran into a corner, his ears flat, and a strange new, threatening sound came from his throat.

"Daisy," Tom said, "you'll have to get Rufus away from here. I'll distract the dog and you must run as fast as you can."

"But where shall I go?" Daisy cried.

"As far as you can towards the west, away from the sun. Glyn's farm is that way. Perhaps he can help." Tom tore off his anorak and threw it over the cub: for a moment the little animal struggled, then he went limp. Perhaps he knew they were trying to help him. Tom thrust the subdued bundle into

Daisy's arms. "Run, Daisy!" he said. "Just keep running. I'll follow you later!"

The sound of barking drew closer. Tom opened the door and shouted, "Run for it, Daisy!" Daisy tore into the trees.

Almost before she'd disappeared the big dog came bounding towards Tom. Tom was terrified, but, keeping his eyes on the dog, he picked up a stick and flung it into the house. Bugle crashed after it, barking furiously. Tom slammed the door and pulled it tight.

Daisy would be safe for a while and, if Tom distracted the Moodys, by the time they found their dog, Bugle would have lost the fox's scent.

He ran away from the stone house, through a thicket and into a clearing where he could easily be seen. He gave a loud whoop!

Branches snapped in the distance. There was an angry shout as Brian and his brother tried to locate his voice. He saw a flash of colour through the trees and then Brian shouted,

"Tom Turner, is that you?"

Tom ran. First he raced towards the sun, drawing the Moodys away from Daisy. He might not have been a country boy but he was smaller and faster than the others. He hid in the thick shoots of a hazel bush and watched Brian and his brother thunder past. When they had disappeared, Tom doubled back, keeping low, careful and quiet, until he was sure the Moodys were out of earshot. And then he ran. He ran through a part of the wood that he'd never explored: thicker and darker, tangled with brambles, pitted with holes, strewn with grass-covered tree-stumps. He kept going, away from the sun now, hoping to find a path, a road or a house. There were no sounds in the wood. Perhaps the Moodys had given up the chase? Once or twice Tom called to his sister. He wondered what had become of her? Has she fallen and lost the cub? Then he found himself climbing a familiar bank and this time, when he called his sister's name, someone answered him.

"I'm here, Tom. Right at the top!"

Tom scrambled up the last few feet and found Daisy grinning at him. Beyond her, across the wide field-patterned plain, lay misty blue mountains.

Daisy's white skirt was covered in grass-stains; her new pink shoes were soaking and her bare arms were swollen with scratches and nettle-stings. There was mud on her forehead and her curls stood out like a tangled yellow brush. "I saved him, Tom!" she said proudly. "Didn't I?"

"Yes," said Tom. "You saved him, Daisy!"

His sister held the little cub out to him and then, before they knew what had happened, she tripped on a tree-root; she toppled forward and the fox fell out of her arms and rolled down into a field on the other side of the bank.

Rufus picked himself up, looked at them and, Tom was quite sure about this, winked. Then he began to run.

"He's not limping!" Daisy cried. "Look!"

Sure enough, Rufus was running straight and smooth; a red arrow flying through the pale gold stubble.

"Will he be all right?" Daisy asked, suddenly anxious. "He's still only a cub."

"A big cub!" Tom said. "He'll be all right. A fox as crafty as that can take care of himself."

They watched the red fox until he merged into the misty distance and vanished, and it was only then that Daisy said, with a bit of a sob, "We're lost. What're we going to do now?"

"We're not lost," Tom said confidently. "I know where we are. I came here, once before, when I was chasing Glyn."

Tom lead the way and Daisy followed. In a few minutes they were in the Bowens' orchard. The farmyard was empty. The house was silent. The Bowens were out, it seemed, so Tom and Daisy found their way to the road and began the long walk home.

When they got back to Hazel Cottage they were surprised to find their parents and all the Bowens in their garden.

"Where have you been?" cried Mrs Turner, running to hug them. "We were all so worried. I rang the Bowens thinking you were there, and we've all been out searching. Good heavens, Daisy, what have you been doing?"

Before either of the children could reply a voice called, "Tom's been keeping foxes in the wood," and they all turned to see Brian and his big brother, Jo, leaning over the fence. "He shut our hound in that old house," Brian said, "but I found this!" And he waved Tom's old sweater. "It's got Tom's name inside," he went on, "and it smells all foxy."

"Our Bugle got the scent all right," said Jo, "went mad he did. You should tell your kids to mind their own business, Mr Turner. Foxes should be killed."

"Not cubs," Glyn muttered. He and Tom exchanged glances and it seemed to Tom that an understanding passed between them.

"It's none of your business, what my children have been doing," Mr Turner told Jo, and then he turned to Tom. "Now what have you been up to, Tom? Where've you been all morning?"

Tom gritted his teeth; one day he would tell his father the truth, but not now. "It's a secret," he said.

And Daisy piped up, "A red secret!"

"You'd better come clean, kids. You've been hiding a ruddy fox, haven't you?" Big Jo shifted his shotgun on to his shoulder.

"Yeah!" Brian muttered menacingly.

Tom and Daisy stood their ground. They glared silently at the Moodys.

"I hope you've got a licence for that gun," Mr Turner said to Jo. "Because unless you leave right now, I'm going to inform the police you've been threatening children with it, and they don't take kindly to that sort of behaviour."

Jo muttered something under his breath, then he and Brian stalked off with a defeated-looking Bugle loping after them.

"Well," said Mrs Turner, "I always say a cup of coffee helps at times like these. Won't you all come in!"

The adults went indoors and Mrs Turner called out, "Clean yourselves up, children, and you *might* get a piece of cake for breakfast!"

But the four children did not immediately follow their parents. They had things to discuss.

"Did you know that puppy was really a fox?" Glyn asked Tom.

"'Course I did," Tom replied. "I'm not that ignorant."

"I'm sorry I tricked you," Glyn said. "I didn't know what else to do. I found the cub in the hedge; he looked so bad. I put him in one of our barns but Bugle came sniffing round, so I thought . . ."

"You thought you could pretend your mum had sent us a puppy and because we were townies, we wouldn't know the difference," Tom said, almost angrily.

"Sorry," Glyn murmured. "I had to find someone to look after him."

"Well, we did," said Tom, "but my dad's not stupid, you know. I had to keep the fox in the woods where no one would see him."

"And did you save him from Bugle?" Megan asked.

"Daisy saved him," Tom said.

"Daisy?" the Bowens exclaimed together, gaping at Daisy.

"Yes, she ran through the wood carrying him while I shut Bugle in the stone house. D'you know that crafty cub could run by himself," Tom went on, "he wasn't lame at all, he just knew he was safer with us."

Daisy suddenly launched into an account of her adventure, and to

Tom's amazement, Megan listened intently and moved closer to his sister. Then the two girls were walking through the front door together, hand in hand.

"My sister talks too much," Tom said.

"She can keep a secret though," Glyn was gazing after Daisy with admiration, and then he looked at Tom and added, "A red secret!"